HarperCollins®, ✚®, HarperFestival®, and Festival Readers™
are trademarks of HarperCollins Publishers Inc.
Stuart Little: A Little Too Fast
Text and illustrations copyright © 2004 by Adelaide Productions, Inc.
Printed in the U.S.A. All rights reserved.
Library of Congress catalog card number: 2003101721
www.harperchildrens.com

1 2 3 4 5 6 7 8 9 10

First Edition

# STUART LITTLE™

## A Little Too Fast

*Adaptation by Laura Driscoll*
*Based on the teleplay by David Slack*
*Illustrations by Thomas Perkins*

HarperFestival®
*A Division of* HarperCollins*Publishers*

Stuart and George were so excited.

They were going to spend

a whole day at the fair!

Even Snowbell wanted to join in

the fun.

*There might be food there*, he thought.

They had a map.

They had tickets for rides.

The only question was:

What did they want to do first?

"Everything!" said George.

"But if we're going to do everything, we need to go fast!" said George. They ran over to the race cars.

They hopped on the Spinning

Saucer ride.

"Faster!" yelled Stuart,

as George spun them around.

They zipped from ride to ride.

They went so fast,

George did not realize that

he had dropped some tickets.

"Hey! Wait!" a guard called

after them.

"Is he talking to us?" asked George.

"I don't think so," replied Stuart.

So they ran off . . .

The line for the roller coaster

seemed to go on for miles.

"This is taking too long!"

said George.

Then the Ferris wheel stalled.

At this rate, George and Stuart

would never get to all of the rides!

And later, Snowbell ran off after a
pretty kitty.

Stuart and George ran after him.

"Snowbell, stop!" shouted Stuart.

"We don't want to lose you."

They didn't have time for this.

Suddenly, Snowbell turned back.

The pretty kitty *wasn't* a cat.

It was a dog!

Snowbell jumped into George's arms.

*"Oof,"* said George.

Stuart went flying.

*"Ahhhh!"* yelled Stuart.

He flew all the way over

to the log ride.

*Splash!*

He landed in the water.

Oh, no . . .

Stuart was headed for the falls!

"Help!" Stuart called out.

George dashed over.

"Grab my hand!" he said.

But Stuart couldn't reach.

So George pulled out

the roll of tickets.

He flung it out like a rope.

Stuart reached . . .

and grabbed on!

*Phew!*

Stuart was safe.

But the tickets were lost.

"Now all of our tickets are gone.
We haven't even done
*half* of the stuff at the fair,"
said George.

Stuart nodded.

"And we've been in such a hurry.
We didn't really enjoy anything
we did do," he said.

Just then, a guard came over.

It was the same guard

George and Stuart saw earlier.

"Are we in trouble?" asked Stuart.

"Did we do something wrong?"

asked George.

The guard laughed.

"No, you didn't do anything wrong,"
he said.

"You just dropped these!"

He handed George the lost tickets.

"Wow! Thanks!" said Stuart.

Now they could enjoy more of the fair.

This time, they decided to take it slow.

Well, mostly.